"I dedicate this book and all things to the Creator,
the source of all creativity, intelligence and existence.
May we all merge with that within our own selves
and be one."

SACHIN MAYI

L!ES
FOR THE
ENTIRE
FAMILY

SACHIN MAYI
AUTHOR

SUSANA EDERY
DESIGNER

JUAN PABLO BARRIOS ROA
ILLUSTRATOR

DR. BINDU MAYI, VIVIAN ROULEAU
EDITORS

Royal Teas

Every country is proud of, and honors her great inventors, and England is no different. Great inventors make a country look good and smart, too. Most countries honor their great inventors with a Nobel Prize and a nice monetary award, but England went the extra mile. England had a unique way of honoring her inventors with more than just a Nobel Prize plaque to stick on the wall. The greatest honor you could have as an Englishman, besides winning a bar fight after a few drinks, was to have tea with the Queen, and inventing something exceptional was one of the ways of getting there.

When someone in England came up with a great invention, of which the English have had many including the hard tips of shoe laces that make it easier to get them in the holes, coffee cup handles to keep your fingers from burning on a nice cup of hot tea, butterfly nets and the like, the Queen would have them in for tea. Sir Isaac Newton who developed the Newtonian telescope, the law of Gravity, the law of motion, and other useless discoveries, described tea with the Queen as a royal affair. Doors would be opened, coats taken by gentlemen in white gloves, everybody proper and well dressed. It was an experience you could only dream about or see in an old English movie like 'Gone With the Wind'. The experience was so far removed from normal English life, and so special, that people went to great lengths to invent something that would capture the Queen's attention.

One bloke (English for chap) wanted so badly to meet the Queen that he spent 60 years of his life inventing everything he could imagine, and still didn't get to see her. Today, there is a section of the British Museum in England dedicated to him and his thousands of useless inventions. But for those who were more fortunate and more intelligent, or perhaps just luckier, it was off to tea with the Queen. She would, of course, give each of them a dust-collecting plaque and would present them with a sizeable cash reward as well.

But it was the privilege of taking tea with her that meant the most to the Englishmen, and the stories would frequent many a bar scene long after the money was gone and the plaque was covered with dust somewhere. This privilege of taking tea with the Queen did not endure, however. In the late 19th Century, this custom was discontinued for security reasons. What remained from this custom was the invention of the word "royalties," which, believe it or not, the Queen invented herself.

roy · al · ties

1.   The granting of a right by a monarch to a corporation or an individual to exploit specified inventions.

2.   A share in the proceeds paid to an inventor or a proprietor for the right to use his or her invention or services.

(Note: the tradition of awarding royalties to inventors has been adopted by almost all modern nations, but ever since the day the Queen stopped having tea with the English inventors, not one invention has come out of England.)

The End

Camel Flogging

In the early days, long before the Animal Protection League and the National Humane Society for Animals, there was a time when animals were fighting for survival like the rest of us. It was survival of the fittest, and every animal was basically trying to eat or not be eaten by the other. As time went on, a natural hierarchy emerged. Stronger and smarter animals started rising to the top of the food chain, and the smarter ones began dominating the others.

Man would emerge as the smartest of all the animals, and because he held such a prestigious title, he took it upon himself to rule the rest of the creatures on this beautiful but not always so friendly planet earth. This was quite the undertaking for early man as you might imagine. In the same way that early man had to find out what foods were okay to eat and which were poisonous, he also had to find out which animals he could tame and which ones he couldn't. His approach was simple and rather risky. He tried to whip, slap, prod, nudge, tweak and flog the animals into submission. These were early forms of training animals and have since been replaced with positive reinforcement methods. Imagine Siegfried and Roy without their lion whips. The animals were not mistreated for fun but rather as an attempt by early man to domesticate them. You see, animals such as dogs, cats, birds, elephants, camels, donkeys and the like were not always the domesticated creatures that they are today. These animals were wild and free like the animals you see at the zoo, except without the cages.

But early man needed help with various things around the hut and took it upon himself to see which animals would be suitable as pets. He tried to domesticate everything from lions to gerbils, and over the course of thousands of years was able to train a small fraction of the world's creatures. Did you know that most of the animals in the world are still wild? And did you know that current estimates of the total number of species on Earth range from 5 to 30 million? Maybe man isn't as smart as we thought. If it took him millions of years to

domesticate just a handful of critters, imagine how long it will take to domesticate all the rest. Once man found a suitable animal with the right temperament, its training consisted of flogging with long sticks or branches. This created fear and discomfort in most animals and anger in many others. Did you know that you can only flog a tiger once? And other animals, like the blue whale, were too big to be affected by floggers, while others, like the cheetah, were too fast and therefore couldn't be captured to be trained. There was some early footage of a caveman trying to domesticate an earth worm, but it was recorded on the wall of a cave, and the cave collapsed in the early 16th century. Just as kids change their behavior when they get a spanking, flogging animals to try to get them to do work also changed their behavior. Earth worms began to live underground. Monkeys began to live up in the trees. Fish learned how to breathe underwater and ostriches started sticking their heads in the ground although, that didn't help them much.

One of the most amusing changes happened with the camel. Camels were not the smartest of creatures, but they were the smartest when it came to avoiding being flogged. Well, so they thought. They couldn't go underwater or fly far away but they hated being flogged so much that over thousands of years they developed the ability to run deep into the desert to try and escape man. In order to do this, the camel developed some very unique features, which it still has today. One was the hump, which acted as a storage tank for water and also helped the camel to blend in with the sand dunes. But when this wasn't enough blending to keep them hidden from man, who followed them into the desert, nature kicked in and helped. In an evolutionary attempt to avoid getting flogged, the camel began to merge with its environment and went from a beautiful red color to the color of the sand in order to better hide in the desert. You probably didn't know this, but the original camels were not tan but rather a bright reddish color. The color was beautiful and stood out nicely against the sand of the desert. Standing out, however, is not always good – just ask any chameleon, who by the way, has been impossible to domesticate even to this day.

Evolution, that thing that nature created to allow everything in the universe to increase its chances of survival, performed this miracle on the camels. Sadly, camel flogging continues to this day, and man continues to try to domesticate this simple but stubborn creature. But they can't be all that dumb because we now have a word for the camel's valiant attempt to hide found in the modern dictionary:

cam · ou · flage
from camel*flog*ging

1.   the act, means, or result of obscuring things to deceive an enemy, as by painting or screening objects so that they are lost to view in the background, or by changing colors to blend with the desert to avoid being flogged.

The End

See Saw

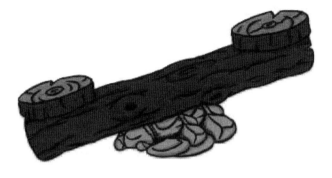

Latvia is no different from any other fishing country in Eastern Europe. The fathers work off the coast fishing, the mothers stay at home and cook and clean, and the children play. Girls grow up to be mothers themselves, and boys grow up to be fishermen like their sas. That's right "sa." Sa is the slang term for father in Latvian, from the word safascha.

As a small country, Latvia depends on its fishing industry for its survival, and being small it also depends on the well-being of its people to keep the population growing and flourishing. Because of this, Latvian boys were not allowed to be close to the dangers of the sea while their fathers were fishing until they were 15 years of age. Latvians, being somewhat poor and living in an under-populated country, knew that losing boys to the sea was not good for business. But boys will be boys, and boys like to hang out with their sas.

If you have ever seen the coast of Latvia, you will have noticed that the sea is bordered by a long ridge. The boys were neither allowed to be on the ridge, or beyond it by the sea. But their fathers were right there on the other side, and the boys wanted to be with them and see what they were doing, and marvel at the fish they were catching. Latvians are not rocket scientists, and they didn't come up with amazing inventions like the English, but thanks to the Latvian boys Latvia is still known today for its simple yet world famous invention. With what little resources they had, the boys made use of large stones and trees to create a device that would allow them to look over the ledge to see their sas, and this is how it worked. The boys balanced the tree or board on the stone, and with a boy on either side they would create a momentum, up and down, that would allow the boy on the side facing the sea to rise up and look over the ledge to see what his father was doing. Being kids, every time, and I do mean every time, the boy facing the sea would be up, the other boy would ask him, "See Sa? See Sa?"

It was a matter of centuries before this clever, yet simple game was brought back by missionaries to the much advanced and much wealthier United States where boys now have computers and cell phones and hardly even see their sas, much less play on a seesaw. But you can still find seesaws on some local school play grounds, although generally lacking the amazing view that you would have seen on the Latvian coast.

see · saw

1. (also known as a teetertotter) is a long, narrow board suspended in the middle so that, as one end goes up, the other end goes down...

The End

On the Flip Side

If you are cool, or ever wanted to be cool, and are over the age of 40, you may have used the expression, "Catch you on the flip side". This catchy phrase originated in the 1950s and was coined by a man whose fame would go on to become legendary. Although he coined the phrase, it was actually an admirer of his who first used the phrase on him. Back then, flip side referred to the backside of a seven inch vinyl record on which singles were released. It was an era when listening to records, juke boxes, and going to dances were very popular. It was also a time when this incredibly handsome and talented young singer from Memphis started to gain popularity. He was so popular in fact that when he attended an event, every girl would clamor to have a dance with him. One girl was so enamored by him that she wanted to have all of his attention to herself. It was during one of these moments at a dance that she used this line on him. They were dancing and she could see that there were other girls waiting nearby who had been promised the next dance. Before her song ended, and the record was being flipped in the jukebox, she whispered in his ear in the sexiest voice she could muster, "Catch you on the flip side?" in order to try and secure the next dance. She didn't get that dance, as the girls waiting for a turn wouldn't stand for it. But her phrase turned out to be the best line that a good southern boy could use to politely put at bay all the

ladies waiting, and he went on to use it frequently. Whereas it initially held promise of a future dance, the phrase went on to popularly refer to the concept of a casual see you later (maybe). This certainly became the case with the man who often used the phrase but could not have possibly danced with all the women who wanted his attention. By now you probably guessed that his name was Elvis Presley, and his phrase would go on to be heard on such television shows as "Happy Days", and in the movies "Caddy Shack" and "Gone with the Wind".

PS. The lady who really coined the phrase went on to write a song called "Catch You on the Flip Side" which was about Elvis but was never released. Her name was Anne Murray and she is reported to have been "The King's" all-time favorite female singer.

The End

Tooth of the Lion

If you were on a trivia game show, and for $10,000 you had to guess which flower's name means Tooth of the Lion, would you be $10,000 richer? If you read this story you would, because the answer is "dandelion." But do you know its origin, not for more money, just for fun? Its origin is French:

Dent = tooth

De = of the

Lion = Lion (of course)

But what crazy person named this little yellow flower that turns your nose yellow when you smell it, tooth of the lion? It looks nothing like a lion's tooth even from a distance. It doesn't have anything to do with lions. And dandelions and lions don't even exist in the same geographic region. Well, that didn't matter to King Louis III

of France but that was because King Louis III did in fact become crazy. His craziness was a by-product of a disease not uncommon in those days and which was generally curable. But King Louis, being a proud king, would not admit to being sick and avoided the stigma as well as the cure. And crazy he became. So much so that he began hallucinating—a lot! He hallucinated about many things, and many of them scared him too. Unplanned hallucinating is not fun for anyone, but imagine how difficult life could be if you were a hallucinating king. You are trying to tell so many people under your command what to do and you are seeing things that they are not. The king's courtiers had the worst of it since it was their job to support him and carry out his commands, crazy or otherwise. This became quite the undertaking, never knowing what their king was going to spring on them from day to day. But they loved their king dearly. He was always very kind and generous to them, and they did their best to support him.

If you have ever seen French castles, you would note that they are surrounded by the most beautiful flower gardens. Walking in these flower gardens was a favorite past time of King Louis until that dreaded day that would keep him housebound until his demise.

That day, King Louis thought he saw the most dreadful lion hiding in the garden amongst the roses and philodendrons. He even pointed out the lion's frightful teeth to the servants, directing them to look at these cute little yellow flowers and saying, "Look there, the dents de lion," French for lion's teeth, and he ran into the castle.

Hiding behind his royal curtains, and peaking out fearfully, the king could not rest. He asked his courtiers to call in expert hunters to rid the garden of the lion. The courtiers obeyed their king to the best of their ability, and the hunters removed the lion, one tooth at a time. They held the teeth up to show the king, who stayed in his castle where he was barely brave enough to watch from his royal terrace. He shuddered at the sight. Because he was so afraid that there were more lions hiding in his gardens, the king never left the castle again. To protect his visitors, he instructed his courtiers to put signs up in the garden reading "Beware of the Dents de Lions!" The clever courtiers, knowing the signs were too far away for the king to read, and not wanting people to think their king was in fact mad, wrote in small letters "Beautiful Dandelions!" instead on the sign. Dandelions are known for their medicinal qualities and blossomed every year in the garden, so the courtiers decided to send them to the market to be sold rather than have them go to waste. The King's Council, wanting their king to be remembered in the best light, decided to send the proceeds from the sales to the poor on behalf of the king. It was a strange way to make the king a philanthropist and a stranger way to forever change the name of a little yellow flower. But they will still turn your nose yellow and the greens are actually good to eat.

The End

flouride

Fluoride is the substance that toothpaste manufacturers began promoting 60 years ago to boost toothpaste sales. It is still used in toothpastes today and was named after Sebastian de la Florida of Spain, a scientist by trade. But this whitening chemical was not the only thing named after him. He had a marshy land, discovered by Juan Ponce de Leon while searching for the Fountain of Youth in 1513, named after him as well. Here is the story of how it all came to pass.

Juan Ponce de Leon discovered America when he landed on the shore of southeastern USA at what we now know as Florida. Juan and his men were looking for something very special, the mystical fountain whose waters would preserve the youth of anyone who drank of it. They found that this land was filled with beautiful palm trees and wonderful beaches, the aspects of Florida that are

treasured today by both residents and tourists alike. But these were not the treasures that Juan Ponce de Leon and his men were looking for. Juan was determined to find the fountain of youth and after some time he was sure that he had found it. His excitement waned quickly however when he found out that there were numerous alligators swimming around in his treasured fountain. Florida was a swampy marshland and was, and still is, home to many alligators. Even today people have to be careful about any open body of water in Florida besides their own swimming pool because there is a good chance an alligator or two may reside there. Juan wanted to do his experiments on the water, and the presence of alligators was making his research a bit too treacherous. If he was going to impress anyone back home with the fountain's healing properties, he would need to rid this marsh of its predators enough to get the pure samples that he needed. This led to an all out battle between his men and the gators. The battle lasted for almost two years and cost Juan Ponce de Leon the lives of half of his men.

Alligators are great at hunting and even better at surviving. As a matter of fact, they are one of the creatures on the planet today that have lasted since the early dinosaur age. But Juan persisted tooth and nail, and after two years, succeeded in collecting his samples from the fountain of youth. Having what he wanted, Juan and his surviving crew packed up their gear and set sail home to Spain to report his findings. Not wanting to show up with only water from his trip, and needing to have a reason why it took him two whole years to return, Juan decided he better bring the heads of the killed alligators with him to lend credence to his story.

In spite of his amazing discovery, his return did not go well. Juan was reprimanded by the Spanish Court for bringing back outlandish stories and reptile heads instead of gold, treasures, and conquered new lands. As Juan was trying to plead his case and get someone—anyone, to listen to his story about the discovered magical fountain, he kept noticing all the magistrates staring at the alligator heads. Ignoring Juan, the magistrates began whispering amongst themselves and soon they all were staring fixedly at the alligator heads. Juan was confused. He heard them talking about the alligator teeth and was very surprised to find that the Spanish government seemed more interested in the teeth of the alligators than they did in the fact that one of their great explorers had found new land and a magical fountain. Juan kept holding up the water, but no one listened or cared. It turns out that the Spanish Court was mesmerized that these gators had some of the whitest teeth that anyone had ever seen, and certainly ever seen in the mouth of a wild animal. They stopped the meeting and had the teeth sent to the Royal Laboratories immediately. The teeth were examined by the scientist Sebastian de la Florida who found that the alligator teeth were covered by a natural chemical that kept them shiny and white. This chemical was fluoride. Fluoride would have perhaps been Juan Ponce de Leon's most famous discovery since it originated from his explorations overseas, but the Spanish government dismissed him without any recognition and told him that he could go back and continue his research if he wanted to. The Spanish Court knew that they had found a substance that could bring them much fame and wealth. They were happy. Juan of course was in utter disbelief, so he hesitated and asked unbelievingly, "Is that all?" The court looked at him and then looked at Sebastian de la Florida holding the alligator's beautiful white teeth. They smiled at Sebastian knowing that their own teeth would soon be shiny and white and then turned back to Juan and replied, "Oh, yes, and you can name the new land Florida." And so it was.

Note: Juan Ponce de Leon did in fact find the fountain of youth and would stay young and healthy well into his 100's. Towards the end of his life he was often heard mumbling something about those stinking alligators. Somewhere in Florida, the alligators guard the precious fountain to this day. If you happen to find it, you may want to leave the alligators behind when reporting your discovery.

fluoride

1.   Fluoride is the anion F-, the reduced form of fluorine. Fluoride is found naturally in low concentration in fresh water where certain reptiles are known to inhabit.

The End

Pair of Medics

In the late 1400's, Queen Isabella of Spain invented a practice that would later become known as the ambulance. It started, however, not with big trucks with flashing lights and sirens, but rather with just people. They were called ambulanciatas. Ambulance comes from the Latin word ambulare, which means to walk. The ambulanciatas were the ones who were charged with going onto the battlefield and rescuing injured soldiers who were still capable of walking. This went on to become a worldwide practice for transporting the injured off the battlefield until the early 1800's when, starting in London, the transport carriage was introduced. Ambulances then, as now, were equipped with a pair of medics who packed in as much medical equipment as they could to treat the injured on the spot, and then transport them to the hospital for further medical treatment. One medic could also treat the patient while the other one drove. The ambulance was fictitiously portrayed with three drivers in the humorous movie "Mother, Jugs and Speed" starring Raquel Welch as . . . well, not Mother.

Today ambulances no longer help people walk. Instead the injured are placed on a stretcher and loaded inside for transport, making the name ambulance a misnomer. It is for this reason that in the United States today we see the name ambulance being replaced by the name Paramedics on the side of the vehicles.

The name Paramedics was derived from "Pair of Medics", referring to the two medics in the ambulance arriving at the scene of the accident.

It was only coincidental that the word para, meaning before, and medics, meaning doctors, wound up being the new name. The ambulanciatas of today are not doctors, they are the before doctor guys. They are trained to keep you alive until you get to the real doctors.

And just as a footnote, there was a dramatic decline in the use of ambulances when only a pair of medics would show up and no Raquel Welch.

The End

from the Gecko

It is strange to think that a phrase that means "from the beginning" doesn't have a beginning at all, or at least not a beginning that is recorded or traceable in any way. But if you research back how far this phrase actually goes, you will not only understand why it doesn't have a traceable beginning, but you will discover some other amazing facts as well. The phrase as we know it today is "from the get go," meaning right from the beginning. Some examples are: Person A asks, "How long have you parted your hair in the middle?" Person B replies, "From the get go." And he pulls out a picture of himself when he was a baby with his hair parted in the middle. Or, person A says, "I have lived here for 70 years, has that mountain always been there?" Person B says, "From the get go," and then mumbles something about senility under their breath. But where did this phrase actually originate, and what is this whole "get go" thing? Interestingly, the phrase originates from the time before time. It originates with our ancestors the cavemen, and like all things from the past, this phrase has morphed over time. You may have played the parlor game where you line up several people, and the first person whispers something in the next person's ear and he is supposed to whisper the same thing in the next person's ear, and so on down the line, and then by the time the last person hears it and blurts it out, it is something totally different. Well that is pretty much how the cavemen lived on a daily basis. But this one particular phrase was particularly dear to them. The Troglodyte, or caveman, used the phrase "from the gecko," and this is what it meant.

During the Paleolithic era, in the region that is known today as New Zealand, a species of gecko known as Delcourt's gecko existed alongside the Troglodyte. This gecko was the largest gecko known at the time and it was also unique among lizards in its vocalizations. It was revered by the cavemen as not only their protector, but also as their source of wisdom. It was the medicine man who would communicate with the gecko. He would do this while under the influence of various hallucinogenic herbs, which the gecko also ate. During this ceremony, the medicine man dressed up like the gecko, and once a month, or whenever necessary, he would talk to the gecko about tribal matters asking the gecko if they should do this or that. If the gecko said yes, the medicine man would inform the chief who then told one tribe member, who then told another one, and down the line. One tribesman sat close by listening in to one of these private sessions to hear what the gecko's voice sounded like when it spoke their language. Not only did he report not hearing the gecko speak their language, he said that he didn't hear the gecko say anything at all. The medicine man, however, was heard speaking at length to the gecko about all sorts of things and even threw in some jokes and had a hearty laugh from time to time. These sessions marked the beginning of many new practices, beliefs and customs. And if anyone who hadn't heard the gecko's new instructions asked why they had to do a particular thing, such as lowering the toilet seat after use, or floss

ing around their tooth, the response of course would be, "from the Gecko". Like the parlor game we mentioned earlier, and as this was a time of oral rather than written communication, the instructions from the gecko to the medicine man to the chief to the people got misquoted as time went on. Many of the traditions that we have today are the result of such miscommunications. One of the most amazing examples of this is man beginning to walk upright on two legs instead of using all four limbs to walk.

Long after the original members of the tribe had died off, and there were no longer medicine men eating funny herbs and talking with large lizards, and as time and oral traditions would have it, the phrase from the gecko, which had little meaning in other parts of the world, became the phrase we use today, "from the get go". The phrase did mean then and still means now, "from the beginning."

It is interesting to note that a well known insurance company uses both the caveman and the gecko in its advertisements and have been doing so from the gecko. . . I mean, get go. I guess some of us are still taking advice from geckos.

The End

Vespa

Have you ever wondered how bugs got their names? Fly is obvious, but what about mosquito and cockroach? And where did names like beetle and bumblebee come from? Bees do seem to bumble around, but that doesn't explain the bee part. Did you know that bumblebees, the fat black and yellow ones, are one of the great mysteries of science? Because bumblebees have tiny little wings and big fat bodies, it should be physically impossible for them to fly, but they do and that may explain the bumbling. Insect names are strange, and it may be worth studying their origins. It will most likely lead you to some scientist who discovered the critter, and then was granted naming rights. In this instance you may find out that he named the bumblebee after his fat and bumbling Aunt Bee. But in spite of their strangeness, the names I mean, not the scientists, the world has gone on to use many of these names on consumer products. Some examples are Bumblebee Tuna, Volkswagen Beetle, Burt's Bees, and many others. Italy is no foreigner to the use of insect names on products as well. You may be familiar with one of its most famous ones, the growingly popular Vespa. Vespa, Italian for wasp, is a line of scooters invented by Rinaldo Piaggio. The Vespa Company began in Florence, Italy, in 1946, but the Vespa was not designed to be a vehicle for the people like the Volkswagen, which was promoted into production by Adolph Hitler. Volkswagen, in fact, means "vehicle for the people."

The Vespa was created for an Italian Special Forces group known as the GIS. The GIS, a division of the Carabinieri police force, is a group specially trained in counter-terrorism operations with emphasis on marksmanship. They are like S.W.A.T and are called in when the police are not enough for the job. Because of the precarious nature of their work, the GIS wanted a unique vehicle to use on their special missions and they hired retired fighter-plane engineer Rinaldo Piaggio to come up with a solution. Mr. Piaggio was given an extensive budget to create the ideal, fully equipped, motorized tactical defense vehicle, and he in fact came up with something totally amazing. His vehicle had everything: extensive weaponry and gadgets, multi-terrain functionality, bullet proof armor plating, and even a laser. Piaggio determined that this would serve every need of the GIS and more. He couldn't wait for the day to show it off. Mr. Piaggio dressed up in his finest suit and rode up on another invention of his, a simple scooter. When he approached the hangar where his masterpiece was being stored, the GIS officials were also arriving. They walked up to him, looked over the scooter, shook his hand and said it was perfect. The scooter, being small, quiet and quick, would allow the GIS to maneuver into risky situations relatively undetected, and could easily go through narrow passageways and over rough terrain. There is reportedly a photo of that famous handshake and the surprised look on Piaggio's face. He never did

get to show them the one with the laser on it, which remains an unused military masterpiece to this day. It took Piaggio all his time and effort to put the scooter into production for the GIS. It was not Piaggio, however, who would go on to name this scooter Vespa, Italian for wasp. The Special Forces named it Vespa because it not only looked like a wasp from the front, but it also represented the vehicle being used in sting operations. It was a coincidence within a coincidence. It was later in 1947 that Piaggio, maintaining the copyrights to the design, would start to make the scooter available to the general public. He kept the name Vespa, which you can add to your list as you research products named after insects.

The End

Goodyear/Goodrich

Many entrepreneurs have fascinating stories behind their successes, and the original tire manufacturers of Goodyear were no exception. Their success resulted from an interesting combination of optimism and market street smarts. The company was founded by Frank Seiberling and friends in Akron, Ohio, in 1898. This group of young entrepreneurs actually knew very little about tires. However, it all began with their great ability to see trends and predict future markets. The future they saw at that time was in transportation, and they were right on. But how to go from insight to being one of the nation's leading companies of the time was where they excelled. None of these guys knew anything about building a car or designing a motor, and wouldn't even if they could. They loved to use their minds instead of their hands and capitalized by adding to the right moment at the right time. What do we mean by adding to the moment? Imagine that someone you knew invented a widget. And you knew everyone would want it and buy one. And you saw that if you added a simple handle to the widget, it would be even better and easier to use. Just by adding the handle, you would become rich from the widget without having to invent it at all or even worry about selling it yourself. That was these guys. They would add the part that goes with the bigger invention that then becomes a gold mine.

Frank and the boys were on the alert to jump on just such an opportunity. They knew that success was a combination of being alert and getting and seizing the opportunity when it arose. So when a gentleman named Henry Ford starting toying with motorized transportation, they were ready.

Prior to this opportunity, Frank's vision was shoes—not for people's feet, but for every other mode of transportation including bicycles and carriages. Frank even dabbled in rubber horseshoes of all things, which creates images in my mind of horses bouncing all over the place! Horseless carriages, the first cars, became a reality in the early 1900's, and Frank was in the right place at the right time. After several pots of coffee and several late nights, Frank and his

friends decided that the tire market was the market to corner. Not
only would it be carried on the wings of great entrepreneurs like
Henry Ford, but it was a renewable market as well. A car would
need to have its tires replaced every so many miles, just like you and
I have to replace our shoes from time to time. It was a combination
of market smarts and optimism that led the young group to name
their tire company Goodyear. The name Goodyear had nothing to
do with tires but rather with this group's optimism for their new
enterprise. Their company's name would prove its weight in gold,

with profits today in the billions of dollars, and would lead the company to create its famous Goodyear Blimp, a masterpiece of marketing genius.

But this was just the beginning for the young and fortune hungry men, because it was these same market smarts that led the group to create the competition tire company, Goodrich. That's right, Goodyear and Goodrich were sister companies with the same owners. It was a simple marketing strategy used by Goodyear to corner the tire industry from all sides. They figured that car owners have to buy tires, so if consumers didn't buy them from Goodyear, then they would be the other guys that they bought the tires from. The strategy worked and both companies sold in the millions. This competitive marketing strategy worked so well in fact, that they would even go as far as to compete with each other publicly, running TV ads saying, "See that blimp up in the sky? We're the other guys!" But in reality, they were not. They were the same guys who knew that Goodyear meant Goodrich!

The End

Temper Pea Dick

We all know the story "The Princess and the Pea" by Hans Christian Andersen. A prince wanted to marry a real princess and used the pea test to find out if she was a true princess by seeing if she could detect the pea which was buried under many mattresses, while she slept.

Well, what we probably did not know is that this romantic pea story actually came from a less glamorous pea mattress story involving not a princess sleeping on a pea, but a prince—Prince Richard to be exact. Spoiled Prince Richard, known as Dick to both his family and enemies, was very much that, spoiled. He was so spoiled that he had to have everything just the way he wanted it. Why not? He was a prince after all! Well, needless to say, it didn't make his craftsmen happy. They were responsible for making and remaking things.

Just like the prince who was looking for the perfect princess, the time came when Prince Dick was looking for the perfect mattress. You see Dick was a really fussy sleeper, a fussy eater, and fussy just about everything, and his mattress had to be just so. How did he test his mattress to see that it wasn't too soft or too hard? That's right, he used a pea. Prince Dick determined in his mind, which was probably not much larger than a pea, that the perfect mattress would be the one that was not so soft that the pea kept him awake, and not so hard that he couldn't even feel the pea. This kept the mattress makers very busy, and it kept spoiled Dick very angry. He had little tolerance for mattress makers lacking proper pea sensitivity and spent much of his spare time yelling at them for not getting it right. Well, the mattress makers bonded in the face of their adversity and came up with a nickname for their nemesis the prince. They called him "Temper Pea Dick" although not to his face. The Prince ended up complaining about his mattresses until he was old and grey, and many a fine mattress was created over this time of trying to please him. But it would be a group of Norwegians who would later create the perfect mattress made out of memory foam that would have probably made the Prince jump for joy. They were completely unrelated to the royal lineage of mattress makers of yore, but do you know what they named their perfect mattresses? Tempur-pedic. If

you buy one and sleep on it with a pea underneath, you'll know why.

The End

Storks

*I*f you have brothers or sisters, or had ever been the type of curious child that asked your parents where babies come from, you probably know that babies are delivered by storks. When we think of these birds carrying babies through the air, we may find this very hard to imagine. The average human baby weighs in between six and eight pounds.

How can a bird, which itself weighs up to 19 pounds and has to make itself lighter than air, carry something as heavy as a baby? Well, storks are unique in many ways. To start with, they are very large. Storks can have wing spans of up to 10.5 feet, almost twice the length of an average adult human. Storks are also unlike other birds whose bones are hollow to make them light in the air. Their bones are filled with a dense porous material that is very strong yet light, similar to some forms of concrete. Storks also have long legs and necks, which allow them to carry objects far away from their wings so as not to impede their flight. But the most unique characteristic about the stork is its ability to lift heavy objects. Storks are the ants of the bird kingdom, lifting 50 times their own weight. Ants can lift 100 times their own weight which is incredible, but they are not flying through the air, they are pushing against the ground, which is much easier. This makes the stork one of the wonders of the world and a master at delivering babies to expecting mothers.

You may wonder if humans are the only ones who get babies delivered by storks. The answer is yes, but it hasn't always been that way. In the past, all the world's animals also had storks deliver their babies. Heavier animals, such as lion and bear cubs, were delivered by the much larger and stronger male stork, and smaller species like squirrel monkeys and bunny rabbits were delivered by the female stork. But as the human population increased, so did the work of the storks, so much so that many of the other animals had to wait very long periods to get a baby delivered. One giraffe on record had to wait eight whole years for just one baby. Humans wait only nine months and have always been first in line before all the other animals. But what effect has this had on the other species? Well, with

more and more humans wanting babies, more and more animals have had to wait for theirs. Even the storks themselves had to wait to get their babies because they were so busy delivering human babies. This has added to the growth of the human population, from 1.6 billion in 1900 to 6.8 billion today. A billion is this many – 1,000,000,000, which if you were counting on fingers and toes, you would need 50 million people and a year and a half to do. With approximately 134 million new human births each year, many animals had to wait so long to get babies that they became extinct. Some on the list were the American Lion, the Giant Short-

Faced Bear, the Woolly Mammoth, the Mountain Deer, the cute little Puerto Rican Shrew, and the Bahaman Barn Owl. But these are only a few of the many thousands of animals that we will never get to meet. Some thought the extinctions were due to extensive hunting and humans destroying the natural habitats of animals, but history books show that it was in fact too much demand on the storks having to deliver too many human babies. We should all take the time to see what animals are on the endangered list, like the cheetah, brown bear and blue whale, and decide whether we want these animals to exist in our future or if we want to end up with a planet of just people and no animals at all. It is really up to us you know.

The End

Watch

You are probably all thinking that it must have been a genius who invented the watch, but was it the same genius who gave it such a stupid name? I mean, what can you possibly see on the thing besides the time? And you can't be serious that someone was supposed to be impressed by a second hand moving, tick, tick, tick…. Oh! It did it again! Tick, tick, tick…..Watch…. it will keep doing it… That's great, thanks!

Well, the guy who invented the first timepiece was in fact a genius. His name was Peter Henlein. But Peter didn't give the watch its name. The name "watch" originated long before that in 742 B.C. from a man whose name has been lost to the records, so we will just call him Bruce. As oral history indicates, it was at this time that the passage of time began to be recorded by more than just looking at the sun. A mechanism was created that could more accurately determine the time of day using the sun. This would go on to be known as the sundial, a device that would reflect and direct the sun causing a shadow to fall on a dial that would be numbered with the times of the day. These would be beneficial in helping people show up on time for work, for lunch, or for fishing trips.

Just before the sundial was invented, however, it was not a device, but rather Bruce who would serve as the timepiece. Bruce was somewhat of a genius as well because after watching and studying the movement of the sun, he determined that if he drew a large circle in the sand on the ground and placed rocks around the circle at exact incremental locations, that he could reflect the sun to indicate times throughout the day. The number of rocks chosen was somewhat random. Bruce had intended to place the number of rocks that corresponded with the number of fingers on his hand. He loaded up his cart with the large rocks and took them to the circle. When he started placing them, he realized that he had miscounted and brought two extra. He hated to have the extra rocks go to waste, and he certainly wasn't going to go all the way back and return them, so he decided what the heck and put all twelve down. This was the random beginning of the twelve-hour day. To determine the time,

Bruce would sit on a hill in the middle of his circle all day long and raise his hands, thereby casting shadows on the rocks. Whenever someone came by and asked him what he was doing, he would say, "watch" and he would stand up and raise his hands toward the sun, causing a shadow to land on the circle of rocks. Depending on where the sun was at that time of day would determine where this shadow landed, and then he would tell the person what time it was by counting the rocks. He eventually painted numbers on the rocks with ox dung, because he got tired of counting them out each time. "Whatever" was the response that Bruce got most often to his display, but as time went on (no pun intended), people began to rely on Bruce to keep them up-to-date and on schedule. Bruce was very impressed with his own intelligence and with his clever invention, but it would be his disgruntled wife who would go on to invent the actual sundial. She became so annoyed with her husband sitting up on that hill all day long pretending to be so important and avoiding his chores that she invented this clever device to relieve him of his responsibilities on the hill. True story!

A Brief History of Time:

B.C.	742	Early man's first cave drawing of the sundial
A.D.	330	Sand glasses became fashionable
	1368	Clock making began in Europe
	1511	The first portable clock was invented
	1730	The first cuckoo clock was constructed in Germany
	1875	The first alarm clock appeared in Germany
	1900	First wrist watches appeared

The End

Stop

In the mid-1900s, the United States was facing a dilemma on two fronts, the devastation of war overseas and the devastation resulting from disorderly driving in cities and towns, but they would only be able to effectively stop one. It was during this time that the U.S. militia was scrambling for recruits to fight in World War II. To speed up the process of getting men out into the field, training had to be reduced to a minimum. In order to make up for the lack of proper war training, the U.S. government came up with a manual that recruits would be required to study as they headed out to fight. The manual was small and easy to carry along with all the other essentials for war. With the use of this manual, the training could also continue in the field. The manual was called Standard Tactical Operating Procedures (S.T.O.P.) and its sym-

bol was a red octagon with the word STOP in white letters written across the middle. The eight sides stood for the eight chapters of the manual: Task Organization, Command and Control, Operations, Air Defense Artillery, Fire Support, Operational Security, Combat Service Support and Safety. The red color represented heart and courage. It was thought that if the soldiers wore this symbol on their uniforms, it would not only remind them to be brave, but also encourage them to be diligent in their study. The goal was to create a coherent functioning force in the field as best they could with the time available.

The military leaders in the field were very strict and put a lot of pressure on the men to perform. So much so that the men, upon seeing the red patch on a fellow soldier's uniform, would stop and think to make sure that they were following the rules set forth.

But the plan backfired. During battle, the hesitation of the men made them sitting targets with these red symbols, like bull's-eyes, on their uniforms, right over their hearts. After suffering a great number of war casualties, the government had to pull the program. But unlike the typical US Government of today, they were determined to not let it all go to waste. The manual remains an integral part of military training even to this day, but has been renamed Tactical Standard Operating Procedure. And the red octagon symbol? That was used by the government to solve the other problem, which was paying for our traffic police!

The End

Dis Stink

Distinct should never be confused with distinctive, which is a good thing, and I will tell you why. Can you guess? That's right, German farts! Germans are some of the best farters in the world, and it is not just because of the beer, it is genetics too. Even German children out-fart the rest of the world's youth.

If you have ever been to a German speaking country, you might know that the German word for "this" is dis. Dis is one of the words used in a great bar game in Germany to this day. The game is played with a group of fellow drinkers, and the object is to try to figure out who just ripped one. The game was invented by Johann Reis, a great German inventor of the late 1800's. Reis, a master fart

detector in his own right, was also known for inventing the artificial ear, the first hearing aid device which is a key component used by the elderly participants for this game. The way the game is played is that when people are gathered at a bar, someone inevitably lets one. That is the starting signal for the game to begin. No one has to force it; farting is just a normal part of German life, particularly bar life. The next step is the most fun. Once you hear the signal, everyone jumps up and starts to smell around each other's butts. You have to be careful not to bump heads with someone if you are too anxious to be the winner. When the lucky, or perhaps not so lucky, player finds the culprit, they will jump up and down pointing at them yelling, "dis stinct, dis stinct!" This singles out the gas releaser of the moment, and the winning smeller gets awarded another round from the bar. This game got so popular that it became the normal bar scene in Germany for many years. As a matter of fact, it got so excessive that some bars had to forbid it due to lack of proper ventilation. For those of you wishing to have your life accomplishments amount to more than just being a member of a fraternity and hanging out in bars, we suggest you go for distinctive.

dis · tinct

1.   clear to the senses or intellect; plain; unmistakable: The smell appeared as a distinct German child.
2.   unquestionably exceptional or notable: such as a distinct smell.

The End

FOOTNOTES:

After reading these amazing stories, many people want to know whether what "they" say really happened. What really are the origins of these words that have become so common in our daily language? Below are the other stories, though often times less intriguing, that we have been led to believe. Mind you, these could be considered merely differences of opinion.

ROYALTIES

I couldn't find any history about royalties other than that there are many kinds of them: non-renewable resource royalties, patent royalties, know-how royalties, trademark royalties, etc. But there is no mention of the Queen or even the English for that matter. We can only assume that when we gained our independence from England, we did our best to erase any ties we had with them in spite of the fact that we stole their language and many of their inventions.

CAMOUFLAGE

If you were to research the origin of the word camouflage, you would not find anything about camels, even though it is clear to both of us that CAMOUL, with a French spelling, has in fact clearly CAMOU-f –L-aged right in there. It is purported to come from the Parisian slang word camoufler which means to disguise. We get a lot of our words in the English language from that neck of the woods, but all we really know for certain is that camels don't speak French and they don't like to get flogged.

SEE SAW

You won't find much history of the word seesaw, due most likely to the isolated nature of Latvia. You will find more mention of its synonym teeter-totter, which I believe refers more to the seesaws that were inland. According to some linguist named Peter Trudgill, the term teeter-totter originates from the Norfolk word tit-termatorter, a word understandably inappropriate for children in any other culture. According to Peter, both teeter-totter (from teeter, as in 'to teeter on the edge') and seesaw (from the verb saw) demonstrate a linguistic process called reduplication where a word or syllable is doubled, often with a different vowel, to indicate repeated activity. Now I don't know about you, but it sounds to me like Peter failed to give credit to the children of Latvia and their ingenious creativity, made up this word reduplication, and tried to sound important so he could get his name in the dictionary.

FLIPSIDE

Flipside or flip side does refer to the B-side of vinyl records, which were released beginning in the 1950s. B-sides were an additional song to the record for added value, but not considered to be the hit song. And although Elvis Presley had the highest number of flip sides or B-sides to be charted in the US Hot 100 at 51, and the most B-sides to reach the Billboard Top 40 numbering 26, our experts can't be sure that he can be quoted using the phrase, "catch you on the flip side," although it was surely someone who looked like him.

DANDELION

According to various sources, the word dandelion is a corruption of the French dent de lion which we already know means tooth of the lion. They say that it is due to the coarsely-toothed leaves, which for those of you have seen the plant know that this is about as far-fetched as the imagination can go without medication or illness. In other words, not likely! The Italian, Spanish, and Portuguese languages also use the same name, tooth of the lion indicating that they too must have had knowledge of King Louis III of France and continued the name in his memory. The French later changed the name of this plant to pissenlit which means to urinate in bed referring to its diuretic properties. The English named it pissabeds. The Italians named it pissalletto and the Spanish named it meacamas. Northeastern Italians got even more creative and named it pisacan, which translates to dog-pisses, because the flowers were commonly found on the side of pavements. I guess there are other folks out there with a creative sense for humor.

FLUORIDE

I am sure that we all know that fluoride is a treatment applied topically to teeth in order to prevent tooth decay. It has been flaunted in toothpaste advertising since forever. But there really is no record of alligators brushing their teeth with it or of the substance being the source of the name of the state of Florida. There probably were alligators in the fountain of youth, but when Juan Ponce de Leon discovered the land on April 2, 1513, he named it after the Spanish term Pascua Florida which referred to the Easter season. At least that is what he probably told his friends in America.

PARAMEDIC

According to the Latin definition, the term paramedic is derived from para (auxiliary) and medical, and means "related to medicine in an auxiliary capacity." But to us laypeople who see two medical guys come out of the ambulance whenever someone gets hurt, it is pretty obvious what paramedic really refers to, and it has nothing to do with auxili anything.

FROM THE GET GO

Merriam and her (or is Merriam a he?) friend Webster, seem to date "get go" back to only 1966, and of course it means "the very beginning" which we already knew, and is used in the phrase "from the get go" which we knew also. Apparently the real origins died off with the caveman, but that is why you have Lies for the Entire Family!

VESPA

The Vespa did evolve from a motor scooter manufactured in 1946 by Piaggio & Co. out of Italy. They are Europe's largest manufacturer of two-wheeled vehicles. The inspiration for these vehicles actually came from the US though, Nebraska to be exact. The Nebraska made olive green Pre-WWII Cushman scooters were in

Italy in large numbers and were used by the US military to get around Nazi defense tactics of destroying roads and bridges. Although the information regarding the origins of the Vespa itself and the Italian Secret Service are highly confidential, that photo of Piaggio meeting them has been seen by many, but is still at large. That really tells the whole story, at least a thousand words worth.

GOODYEAR

The Goodyear Tire & Rubber Company was founded in 1898 by Frank Seiberling, and the first Goodyear factory was opened in Akron, Ohio, in 1898. The company did grow with the advent of the automobile and did start with bicycle tires, rubber horseshoe pads, and poker chips. The name Goodyear however was in honor of Charles Goodyear, who invented vulcanized rubber in 1839. Goodrich apparently was not owned by Goodyear or the same guys, even though both of them have some connection to Charles Goodyear and both of them have roots in Akron, Ohio. Goodrich is named after Dr. Benjamin Franklin Goodrich, M.D. who became an American industrialist in the rubber industry. Goodrich actually predated Goodyear, founding the company that still bears his name, BF Goodrich, in 1870. He had a licensing agreement with Charles Goodyear although they didn't have his name. The two companies, Goodrich and Goodyear, did in fact compete for the tire market, including the ad about the blimp.

TEMPUR-PEDIC

According to the historians, TEMPUR material is a viscoelastic memory foam made from polyurethane that was originally designed by and then abandoned by NASA for use in space. Apparently the astronauts didn't deserve a good night's sleep. The Swedish built on this invention and made this material into mattresses. Then some guy named Dag Landvik, scouting for race horses in Europe, found out about it and decided to create a subsidiary of the Swedish Company that originally started work on this idea. He named it Tempur-Pedic. Dag made the company independent, brought it back to the U.S., and set up headquarters in Lexington, Kentucky, which leads us to believe that he probably found the race horses he was looking for as well!

STORK

In Western culture, the white stork is a symbol of childbirth. It began in Victorian times, when the details of human reproduction were difficult to approach, especially in reply to a younger child's query, "Where did I come from?" "The stork brought you to us" was the tactic used to avoid discussion of sex. However, this folklore built on itself and included storks being the harbingers of happiness and prosperity, and possibly grew from the habit some storks have of nesting atop chimneys, down which it was said the new baby could be imagined entering the house. The image of a stork bearing an infant wrapped in a diaper held in its beak became common in popular culture. The small pink or reddish patches often found on a newborn child's eyelids, between the eyes, on the upper lip, and on the nape of the neck are sometimes still called stork bites. There is no way that this could all just be coincidence. We feel it needs further investigation.

WATCH

According to somebody's records that don't date back as far as our guy on the hill, Peter Henlein created the first pocket watch in 1524. Then Patek Philippe invented a wristwatch in 1868, but only as a lady's bracelet watch, intended as jewelry. Then in 1904, a French watchmaker named Louis Cartier designed a watch for early aviator Alberto Santos-Dumont to be used during his flights. I have found no mention of the origin of the name watch, but if I knew where to tell you to look, you would still find the small hill near the circle of stones that remains the unacclaimed origin of all timepieces, minus the guy.

STOP

There is such a thing as a Standard Operating Procedure for the US Army, but when it comes to tactical, they put that first—Tactical Standard Operating Procedure (TACSOP). I am sure that this has helped save a lot of lives, and they probably didn't wear it on their uniforms. But it is clear to both you and me that TACSOP would not have done much good to stop cars. What does stop cars, however, is the red octagon-shaped sign that we have been conditioned and trained to know means STOP. The eight-sided shape is unique to the stop sign, making it recognizable from either side. And the red color matches the red of the stoplight, which also means STOP. When stop signs originated in Michigan in 1915, they were white with black letters. It took one committee to merge with another to finally standardize the sign we have today, which by the way, has a lot of specifications as you might imagine with two big committees overseeing the darn thing. I am surprised they don't have the signs appearing in triplicate! Too bad we missed the National Conference on Street and Highway Safety (NCSHS) back in the early 1900s; we could have been one of the inventors of the STOP sign.

DISTINCT

This word originates from the Old French distincter, probably to indicate the person who let one rather then the stinker itself and also from the Latin distinctus which probably refers to the stinkiness of the entire group in general. We found no mention of the famous German drinking game in the archives, in spite of the fact that we have seen it with our own eyes on a national geographic special.

If you are like everyone else, you love a good story. Since the dawn of creation, everything has a story about how it came to be.

Whether it is how a camel contributed to a new word in our English language or how a simple childhood past time, See Saw, got its name. These stories add richness to the world that we live in. Add in a creative twist or two, or lie if you will, and you have the makings for a really exciting new world.

Stay tuned for the truth about Santa Claus or any other story that may have been puzzling you.

Sachin Mayi

Visit us at www.sachinmayi.com to offer your suggestions, and keep an eye out for our next edition of **Lies for the Entire Family**.

Sachin Mayi and Tenzin

About the Author:

I legally changed my name to **Sachin** in 1998 when I was given the name by a living Saint in South India where I lived for two years meditating and doing service. Ironically the name means; "embodiment of truth and consciousness." Later my desire to serve those in need, inspired me to found the Share-A-Pet Organization, a national non-profit which provides pet-assisted therapy to individuals in hospitals, nursing homes and children's centers as well as a Pawsitive Reading program in schools. Check us out: **shareapet.org**. I balance it all out as an Assistant martial arts instructor at Florida Aikikai, one of the largest Aikido dojos in the country, where I teach a Japanese martial art of "non-violent" self-defense. I currently live in Fort Laurderdale with my gorgeous and loving wife Dr. Bindu Mayi and our three dogs.

My Illustrator:

I never met **Juan Pablo Barrios Roa** personally, a professional illustrator, dedicated to design and digital art. But I will say that he does some of the most amazing illustrations I have ever seen and captured the essence of these stories perfectly.
I look forward to working with him again on the next edition of Lies for the Entire Family.

My Designers:

Susana Edery mastered the design for Lies for the Entire Family, with the final rendition being tweeked by local designer **Andrew Hoffman**. Check out Susana Edery at www.coroflot.com/susyedery/profile and on Facebook and LinkedIn.

Visit me at **www.sachinmayi.com**